A BALL FOR LITTLE BEAR

By EMILY BROUN

Illustrated by DICK MACKAY

In this Ojibway Indian legend, Big Bear plucked the sun out of the sky and brought it home for Little Bear to play with. He didn't know how not having the sun would affect everyone. He just wanted a bright ball. Can you guess some of the things that happened?

* *

Dewey Decimal Classification: E

Illustrated by Dick Mackay

CADMUS BOOKS

A BALL FOR LITTLE BEAR

by Emily Broun

An
Ojibway
Legend

THIS SPECIAL EDITION IS PUBLISHED BY ARRANGEMENT WITH—
THE PUBLISHERS OF THE REGULAR EDITION
E. P. DUTTON AND CO.
BY
E. M. HALE AND COMPANY
EAU CLAIRE, WISCONSIN

LITHOGRAPHED IN THE UNITED STATES OF AMERICA

Once, a long time ago, when Big Bear was gathering nuts in the forest, he came to an open place where boys were playing ball.

The boys shouted as they chased the bouncing
ball, for their hearts were glad. It was harvest

time in the Ojibway country, and after the
ball game there would be feasting.

Big Bear stood watching the game, swaying first on one foot and then on the other, and thought of his son at home.

"Little Bear would like a ball," he said. "A ball would be better than a bag of nuts."

He tried to catch the ball when it bounced his
way.
But Big Bear was old and fat.
The boys were too quick for him.

He gave up and lumbered off, sadly, until he came to the end of the forest.

There, hanging low above the lake, Big Bear
saw the great round sun!

He picked the sun out of the sky and popped it into his bag.

"Now, Little Bear will have a ball to play with,"
he said, and patted the bag proudly.

Little Bear did not run out to meet his father as usual.

He had waited and watched at the door of their cave until dark. Then Little Bear had fallen asleep.

"I'll just have a nap, myself," yawned Big Bear.
He stretched out on the floor of the cave
with his head on the bag, for a pillow.

It was a very long nap that lasted months and months and months.

Meanwhile, in the Ojibway country, the people and the animals were left with no light but the shining of the stars.

No flowers bloomed, no plants grew.

The marshes were empty of wild rice,

the forest of nuts or fruits.

There was no ball play, no feasting.
Everybody was hungry.

The medicine man tried all his charms but nothing worked against the darkness.

At last the animals called a council.
They sat down in the open place in the forest,
all in a circle.
All the animals, except Big Bear!

Red Fox was the first to speak.

"The important thing," he said, "is to find the sun and put it back in the sky."

Owl hooted. "I like the dark earth as it is. But if you must have the sun," he grumbled, "you'll have to go to Bear's cave to get it. I saw Big Bear take the sun out of the sky. He put it in his medicine bag."

"Who will bring back the sun?" asked Red Fox.

"I will," cried Deer, leaping up. "I am the swiftest runner."

"You can outrun us all," Rabbit said. "But you are too timid. Big Bear wouldn't let you get hold of the sun."

Turtle raised his head out of his shell. "I'll go," he said.

"You're too slow," the animals objected with one voice.

"I'd go," said Crow, "if I had something better than these rusty feathers to wear."

"Get the people to make you a coat," Rabbit suggested.

So the Ojibway people made Crow a beautiful
coat that covered all his rough, black feathers,
except the tip of one wing.

And he flew off to the end of the forest.

Crow stuck his head in the door of Bear's cave, and saw that the bears were asleep. His eyes darted around the cave but there was no sign of the sun.

"The sun is not here," Crow muttered. "Owl
was mistaken."

He was about to leave when Little Bear sat
up and rubbed his eyes in surprise at the sight
of the handsome stranger.

Little Bear did not recognize Crow in his beautiful coat.

"Wake up, Papa!" he cried. "We have important company."

Big Bear stirred and stretched and raised his head from the bag that he had been using as a pillow.

"Oh ho!" thought Crow, and wondered what excuse he could give to look inside the big, brown medicine bag.

Little Bear saved him the trouble.
He eyed the bag hungrily.
"What a lot of nuts you've brought," he said,
and his mouth began to water.

Big Bear rose up. "Anybody could fill a bag
with nuts," he answered. "I've brought you a
ball to play with!"
He opened the bag and drew out the great,
round, dazzling sun.

"Let *me* see it. Throw it to *me*!" begged Crow,
as Little Bear reached for the ball.

"Take good care of it," said Big Bear, throwing it to Crow. "Don't let it roll outside the cave," he cried anxiously. "Don't let it get away!"

But just then Crow gave the ball a push with
his wing and it rolled outside the cave.

And before Big Bear or Little Bear could stop him, Crow flew away with the sun and hooked it back in its place in the sky.

However, as he spread his wings, a wind caught Crow's fine coat,

and whirled it

and twirled it
into a soft, round ball.

Right into Little Bear's arms, it fell —
a ball of his own to play with.